The Four Clever Brothers

A story by the Brothers Grimm
with pictures by Felix Hoffmann

Harcourt, Brace & World, Inc., New York

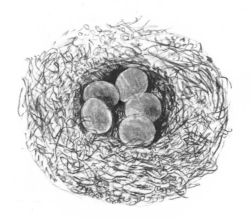

For Klaus

There was once a poor man who had four sons, and they were very dear to him. When they were grown up, he called them together and said: "Alas, my children, I have nothing to give you. You must go out into the wide world and try your luck. Begin by learning a trade and see if you can make your way."

So the four brothers took leave of their father and set out together. After wandering for some time, they came to a crossroads. "Here we must part," the eldest brother said, "but let us meet at this very spot four years to this day. In the meantime, may luck be with us." So each went off in a different direction.

The eldest brother had walked only a short distance when
he met a man who asked him where he was going and what he
intended to do. "I want to learn a trade," he replied.

"Come with me and I will teach you to become a cunning
THIEF," the man said.

"No," replied the eldest brother. "That is not an honest trade, and
what can lie at the end of that road but to be hung on the gallows?"

"Oh," said the man, "you need not fear the gallows, for I will
teach you to steal only those things that no one else cares about."

So the eldest brother let himself be persuaded and learned his trade
so well that soon nothing was safe that he set his heart upon.

The second brother also met a man who asked him where he was going and what he intended to do. "I do not know yet," he replied. "I cannot make up my mind."

"Well, come with me and be a STARGAZER," said the man. "It is a noble calling, and you will learn all the secrets of the heavens."

The second brother liked the idea, and so skilled a stargazer did he become that, when he took leave of his master, he was given a telescope. Through it he could see all that was passing in heaven and on earth. Nothing was hidden from him. The second brother thanked his master, took the gift, and went on his way.

The third brother was apprenticed to a HUNTER, who taught him all the lore of the forest. When the time came for them to part, the hunter gave the young man a gun, and said: "Whatever you aim at with this gun you will be sure to hit." The third brother thanked his master, took the gift, and went on his way.

And the youngest brother, how did he fare? He, too, met a man who asked him where he was going and what he intended to do. "Why not become a TAILOR?" the man asked.

"Oh, no," said the youngest brother, who was, it must be admitted, a rather lazy fellow. "Sitting cross-legged from morning to night, plying a needle in and out, will never suit me."

"Nonsense," said the man. "That is not my sort of tailoring. Come with me and you will learn a different trade."

Because he could not be bothered to think of any more objections, the youngest brother went with the tailor, who taught him all he knew. When he had finished his apprenticeship, the tailor gave him a needle, the sharpest and finest he had ever seen, and said: "With this needle you can sew anything you wish, be it as soft as an egg or as hard as steel, and no seam will be seen." The youngest brother thanked his master, took the gift, and went on his way.

Four years to the day, the brothers met again at the crossroads. They greeted one another warmly and hurried home to their father, to tell him all that had befallen them.

Their father was overjoyed to see them and listened eagerly to their adventures. Then, as he sat with his sons under a tall, shady tree in the garden, he said: "I should like to test how well you have learned your trades." He looked up at the leafy branches above him and said to his second son: "At the top of this tree there is a chaffinch's nest. How many eggs does it contain?"

The stargazer fetched his telescope and, looking through it, saw the chaffinch sitting on her speckled eggs. "Five," he answered.

"Now," said the old man to his eldest son, "see if you can take away the eggs without the bird's knowing."

The cunning thief climbed the tree and took away the eggs, and the chaffinch went on sitting quietly on her nest, without knowing that there were no longer five speckled eggs beneath her soft feathers.

Then the old man took the eggs and placed them on the table that stood beneath the tree—one at each corner of the table and the fifth in the middle—and he said to his third son: "Shoot each of the eggs through the middle with one shot." The hunter fetched his gun, aimed, and fired. And, lo and behold, there were the five eggs, each cut neatly in two.

"Now it is your turn," said the old man to his fourth son. "You are to sew the eggs together again, and also the young birds inside them, so that they are not harmed in any way."

The tailor fetched his needle and stitched the birds and the eggs as his father had directed. When he had finished, he gave the eggs to his brother, the cunning thief, who climbed the tree once more and put them back in the nest without so much as ruffling the chaffinch's feathers.

In a few days' time, the eggs hatched and the young birds crawled out, with only a tiny red streak on each of their necks to show where the tailor had stitched them together.

"I must congratulate you," said the old man to his sons. "You have spent your time well, and I am proud of you. If only your skills can be put to good use, I shall be very happy."

Not long afterwards there was great trouble in the land, for the King's daughter was carried off by an enormous dragon. The King grieved for her night and day and proclaimed that whoever brought her back should have her as his wife.

"This is a matter for us," said the four brothers. "We must try to free her." And each determined to win the Princess for his bride.

The stargazer took his telescope and cried: "I can see the Princess. She is sitting on a rock in the sea a long way from here, and the dragon is by her side."

He went to the King and asked for a ship for himself and his brothers, and they sailed away over the sea until they came to the rock. There sat the Princess, just as the stargazer had said, but the dragon lay with his head on her lap, fast asleep.

The hunter said sadly: "I dare not shoot, for I would kill the lovely maiden as well as the dragon."

"I will try my luck," said the cunning thief. Then he crept up to the Princess and stole her away from under the dragon. So quiet and gentle was he that the beast went on snoring loudly, unaware that he had lost his prize. Full of joy, the eldest brother hurried back to the ship with the Princess, and they steered out into the open sea.

Some time later, when the dragon awoke and found his prisoner gone, he flew after them with all speed, crackling with anger. He hovered over the ship, preparing to land, but the hunter took aim with his gun and shot him through the heart. The dragon fell down dead, but his huge body wrecked the ship. Luckily, the Princess and the four brothers were able to cling to some planks and keep afloat.

They were still in danger of drowning, but the tailor took his wonderful needle and sewed some of the planks together hurriedly with large stitches. Then he climbed onto them and collected the other parts of the ship. These he also sewed together, more carefully this time, and in a short while the ship was whole once more and they could sail happily home.

When the King saw his daughter again, he was overjoyed.

He remembered his promise and said to the brothers: "One of you shall have the Princess for his wife, but you must decide amongst yourselves which it is to be."

Then the four clever brothers began to quarrel, for each had fallen in love with the Princess.

The stargazer said: "If I had not seen the Princess, all your skills would have been useless. So she is mine."

The cunning thief said: "Of what use would your seeing have been if I had not stolen her from the dragon? So she is mine."

The hunter said: "If I had not shot the dragon, he would have slain the Princess and all of you as well. So she is mine."

The tailor said: "And if I had not sewn the ship together with my needle, you would all have drowned. So she is mine."

Seeing that they would never agree, the King said: "Each of you has an equal right, and since you cannot all have the Princess, none of you shall have her, but I shall give to each of you as a reward the quarter of a kingdom."

The brothers knew this decision was fair. "It is better this way than to have us quarrel," they said.

So each received the quarter of a kingdom, and they lived happily with their father for as long as it pleased God.